To Karen and Joyce . . . longtime buddies

LITTLE SIMON
An imprint of Simon & Schuster Children's Publishing Division
1230 Avenue of the Americas, New York, New York 10020
Copyright © 2014 by Henry Cole
All rights reserved, including the right of reproduction in whole or in part in any form.
LITTLE SIMON is a registered trademark of Simon & Schuster, Inc.,
and associated colophon is a trademark of Simon & Schuster, Inc.
For information about special discounts for bulk purchases, please contact Simon & Schuster
Special Sales at 1-866-506-1949 or business@simonandschuster.com.
The Simon & Schuster Speakers Bureau can bring authors to your live event. For more information or
to book an event contact the Simon & Schuster Speakers Bureau at 1-866-248-3049
or visit our website at www.simonspeakers.com.
Designed by Laura Roode
Manufactured in China 0114 SCP
First Edition 2 4 6 8 10 9 7 5 3 1
Library of Congress Cataloging-in-Publication Data
Cole, Henry, 1955- author, illustrator. Big bug / Henry Cole. — First edition. pages cm
Summary: Beginning with a bug, various objects are revealed as being big and small in
comparison with other objects on a farm under the big, big sky.
ISBN 978-1-4424-9897-6 (hc : alk. paper) — ISBN 978-1-4424-9899-0 (ebook)
[1. Size—Fiction. 2. Farm life—Fiction. 3. English language—Comparison—Fiction.] I. Title.
PZ7.C67728Big 2014
[E]—dc23
2013020626

big bug

By Henry Cole

LITTLE SIMON

New York London Toronto Sydney New Delhi

Big bug

Little bug

Big leaf

Little leaf

Big
flower

Little flower

Big dog

Little dog

Big
cow

Little cow

Big farm

Big . . .

Little farm

BIG sky

Little tree

Big
tree

Little barn

Big
barn

Little house

Big house

Little window

Big
window

Little dog

Big dog

Little nap